THE
INVENTION
OF THE
TELEVISION

by Lucy Beevor

raintree

a Capstone company — publishers for children

Raintree is an imprint of Capstone Global Library Limited, a company incorporated in England and Wales
having its registered office at 264 Banbury Road, Oxford, OX2 7DY – Registered company number: 66955

www.raintree.co.uk
myorders@raintree.co.uk

Edited by Jennifer Huston
Designed by Heidi Thompson
Original illustrations © Capstone Global Library Ltd 2018
Picture research by Eric Gohl
Production by Katy LaVigne
Originated by Capstone Global Library Ltd
Printed and bound in Inida.

Original Edition Author
Marc Tyler Nobleman

ISBN 978 1 4747 5285 5
22 21 20 19 18
10 9 8 7 6 5 4 3 2 1

British Library Cataloguing in Publication D
A full catalogue record for this book is availab

Acknowledgements
We would like to thank the following for perm
photographs:
Alamy: Dennis MacDonald, 23, Everett Collection Historical, 16,
17, INTERFOTO, 19 (bottom), Science History Images, 6, 11, World
History Archive, 8; Getty Images: Bettmann, 15; iStockphoto: jack0m,
21; NASA: 4, 5; Newscom: EFE/Miguel Gutierrez, 22, Everett
Collection, 7, Mirrorpix, 9, Oronoz/Album, 13; Shutterstock: 360b, 24
(television screen), Aleks49, cover (bottom right), Aleksandr Bryliaev,
1, Andrey_Popov, 26, BrAt82, cover (top right), Dmitry Naumov, cover
(top middle), Everett Collection, 19 (top), Farhad Bek, cover (bottom
middle), 2, Gino Santa Maria, cover (top left), jakkapan, cover (bottom
left), Monkey Business Images, 24, 27, Perfect Vectors, 20, Scanrail1, 25,
SergeyPhoto7, 14
Design Elements: Shutterstock

CONTENTS

Chapter 1: The first man on the Moon 4

Chapter 2: Before television 6

Chapter 3: Inventors of television 10

Chapter 4: The first television programmes ...16

Chapter 5: Television today 22

Timeline 29

Glossary 30

Comprehension questions 31

Find out more 31

Websites 32

Index 32

THE FIRST MAN ON THE MOON

On 20 July 1969, millions of people around the world tuned in to watch the astronauts of the *Apollo 11* mission land on the Moon. Commander Neil Armstrong was the first man to step onto the Moon's surface. Buzz Aldrin followed a few minutes later. When the astronauts returned home on 24 July, they were welcomed as international heroes. The *Apollo 11* mission was a major success.

As Neil Armstrong set foot on the Moon, he said the now famous words, "That's one small step for man, one giant leap for mankind".

The Moon landing was filmed and **broadcast** around the world. The broadcast set a new world record, as more than half a billion people tuned in to watch the historic event. Even today, that's a lot of people watching one television programme.

The *Eagle* lunar module detached from the main spacecraft to land on the Moon.

broadcast send out a programme on TV or radio
lunar module self-contained part of the larger spacecraft that landed on the Moon

2 BEFORE TELEVISION

Before television was invented, people entertained themselves in other ways. Families sat around the fireplace and told stories. They also read books, sang songs and played instruments. They played card games and board games, such as chess and backgammon. Children also played with wooden toys. In the 1700s and 1800s, a favourite children's game was hoop rolling.

In hoop rolling, the player tries to roll the hoop along the ground by hitting it with a stick.

THE RADIO IS INVENTED

By the late 1800s, the world was changing. People used more machines. The radio was invented in 1895, but for the first 25 years, it was mainly used for sending **wireless messages**. Then on 31 August 1920, the first radio news programme was broadcast in Detroit, Michigan, USA. The British Broadcasting Corporation (BBC) began broadcasting radio programmes every day starting in 1922. The programmes included music, news and other entertainment. Listening to the radio quickly became very popular.

Before television, people listened to the radio for news and entertainment.

wireless message telegraph message sent over a long distance using radio waves instead of wires

THE FIRST FILMS

In the mid-1890s, films were also invented. These moving pictures amazed people. At first, the films showed pictures without sound. They were called "silent films". Musicians played live music to go along with the moving pictures.

In 1927, *The Jazz Singer* became the first successful full-length film with sound. People called films with sound "talkies".

CHARLIE CHAPLIN

Charlie Chaplin was one of the first film stars. He appeared in many famous silent films, including *The Kid* (1921) and *The Circus* (1928).

Charlie Chaplin was a star of the silent-film era.

technology use of science to do practical things, such as designing complex machines

MECHANICAL TELEVISION

The mechanical television was an early idea for sending moving pictures over long distances. In London, in 1926, John Logie Baird of Scotland showed the mechanical television he'd invented. It used a spinning disc that copied a picture line by line. Then each line was sent to another disc. That disc put the image back together.

In 1927, Baird formed the Baird Television Development Company (BTDC). In 1928 the BTDC became the first company to send televised pictures across the Atlantic Ocean between London and New York. The first mechanical TVs went on sale later that year.

John Logie Baird in his workshop

The BBC began broadcasting pictures using Baird's mechanical system. But it was slow, plus the pictures were fuzzy, and they fluttered on the screen. Even so, Baird's work was an important step in the development of television. **Technology** was changing rapidly, and someone needed to find a way to make clearer, faster pictures.

INVENTORS OF TELEVISION

People soon realized that if picture quality was going to improve, televisions would need to be electronic. Philo T. Farnsworth and Vladimir Zworykin were two early inventors of the electronic television. Their work led to the televisions we watch today.

PHILO T. FARNSWORTH

Philo T. Farnsworth was an American electrical **engineer**. When Farnsworth was just 14 years old, he came up with the idea to use electricity to send pictures. Like Baird's mechanical system, Farnsworth's system divided the picture into lines. However, there was one big difference. Instead of spinning discs, Farnsworth believed that he could turn the lines into radio **signals**. The signals could be sent from one place to another using electricity. Then the lines could be put back together to form a picture.

In 1927, Farnsworth filed a **patent** for a camera tube called the image dissector. It was an early version of a television camera. The image dissector could change a picture into a radio signal. That same year, Farnsworth sent the first electronic television picture from the image dissector to a screen in another room in his lab. The picture was a straight line he had painted on a piece of glass.

He lit the picture from behind with a bright lamp. The following year, Farnsworth showed his system to the media by sending a picture of a dollar sign. It was the first working, entirely electronic television system.

Farnsworth holds his image dissector while standing next to his television. He received a patent for the image dissector in 1930.

engineer someone who uses science and maths to design and build things
signal radio, sound or light wave that sends information from one place to another
patent legal document giving sole rights to make or sell a product

VLADIMIR ZWORYKIN

Vladimir Zworykin was an electrical engineer from Russia. He moved to the United States in 1919. Zworykin was working on his own version of an electronic television system around the same time as Farnsworth. Zworykin called his system the iconoscope, and he applied for a patent for it in 1923. Similar to Farnsworth's image dissector, the iconoscope could also change a picture into a radio signal. But Zworykin struggled to make the iconoscope work. Finally, in 1933, he was able to send a picture with the iconoscope. Zworykin received a patent for it in 1938.

Vladimir Zworykin holds an iconoscope.

DID YOU KNOW?

Early inventors used different names for the television. Some of these names were radiovision, radiovisor and televisor.

While he worked on the iconoscope, Zworykin invented a picture tube in 1929. He called it the kinescope. The kinescope was an early television **receiver** – a **vacuum tube** that could receive radio signals. It changed the radio signals back into pictures.

Today, a monument showing Zworykin and his television is on display in Moscow, Russia.

receiver device that receives radio signals and turns them into sound or pictures
vacuum tube glass tube that was used in the past in computers and televisions to control the flow of electricity

LEGAL PROBLEMS

All of these inventions led to the creation of television as we know it today. But the race to make the first working system led to legal problems for Zworykin and Farnsworth. Zworykin worked for the Radio Corporation of America (RCA). RCA offered Farnsworth £75,000 ($100,000) for the patent to the image dissector, but Farnsworth refused. So RCA took Farnsworth to court. RCA tried to say that because Zworykin filed his patent first, Farnsworth's shouldn't be legal. When the legal battles ended in 1939, the court ruled that RCA could sell electronic TVs for home use. But RCA had to pay Farnsworth nearly £760,000 ($1 million) for the rights to make the necessary television parts he'd invented.

Farnsworth shows one of his early televisions. The small square at the top is where the picture was shown.

4 THE FIRST TELEVISION PROGRAMMES

Over time Farnsworth and Zworykin's inventions became popular. But it didn't happen overnight. In the 1930s the first television broadcasts in the United States were fuzzy pictures of dancing and wrestling. Few people even saw these broadcasts because the number of television stations was limited. The number of people who owned televisions was even fewer.

Many new inventions were displayed at the New York World's Fair in 1939.

variety show show with many different types of performers, such as dancers, singers and comedians

16

Many people in the United States saw television for the first time at the 1939 World's Fair in New York. American companies such as General Electric, Westinghouse Electric and RCA showed televisions at the fair. The National Broadcasting Company (NBC) began TV broadcasts on 30 April, the opening day of the World's Fair. That same year, NBC was the first television network to show a baseball game on TV. NBC also broadcast cartoons, game shows, cooking shows and **variety shows**.

People crowded around the television on display at the 1939 World's Fair in New York.

The first black-and-white electronic televisions went on sale in Germany in 1934, followed by the UK in 1936, and the United States in 1938. The first TVs sold for about £150 to £450 ($200 to $600). At the same time, the first TV stations formed. But during World War II (1939–1945), manufacturing of televisions stopped, and it wasn't until after the war that TV became really popular.

NEW FEATURES

By the 1950s, televisions had many new features. The first remote control was available in 1950. The earliest remote controls were attached to the television by a wire. The first wireless remote control came out in 1956. Colour TVs went on sale in 1953.

SUBTITLES

Subtitles, or closed-captioning, is a feature that prints spoken words across a television screen. It was first developed so that hearing-impaired people could enjoy TV programmes. The first closed-captioning system was displayed at the 1971 National Conference on Television for the Hearing Impaired in Knoxville, Tennessee, USA. After several years of tests and the invention of machines to write them, subtitles became more widely available by the early 1980s.

CHANGING STYLES

Television styles have changed over the years. Early TVs had small screens, and their parts were tucked inside large wooden frames. By the 1970s and 1980s, TVs were built with more plastic. They had rounded screens and came in many shapes and sizes.

Many televisions in the 1950s came in large wooden cabinets.

In the 1960s and 1970s, plastic TVs came in all shapes, sizes and colours.

HOW ANALOGUE TELEVISIONS WORKED

Before the 2000s, televisions were **analogue**. Broadcasting stations sent out picture and sound signals. Televisions created pictures and sounds from the signals they received. Picture signals went to the TV screen. Sound signals went to the speakers.

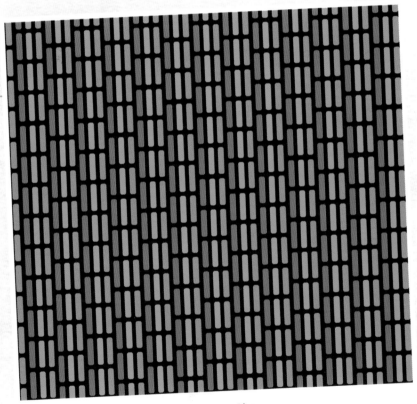

Blue, green and red dots made up the pictures on an analogue colour television.

CATHODE-RAY TUBES

Analogue TVs used a cathode, an anode and a screen to show pictures. These parts made up a cathode-ray tube. A cathode is a heated wire that releases electrons, one of the tiny pieces of an atom. An anode focuses the electrons into a beam. The beam of electrons is shot at the screen, which is coated with phosphor. Phosphor is a material that glows when electrons hit it.

The pictures on an analogue TV screen were made up of dots and lines. The electron beam drew each picture dot by dot, line by line.

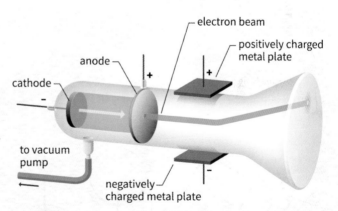

analogue opposite of digital; pictures on an analogue TV are made from dots and lines

5 TELEVISION TODAY

New technology in the 2000s made **digital** televisions possible. Today, most televisions are digital. In the UK, the switch from analogue to digital TV began in October 2007 and was completed in October 2012.

With digital TV, you can choose from hundreds of channels.

A BETTER PICTURE

Digital television uses a digital signal to send pictures and sound. A digital signal is made up of a series of 0s and 1s. This **data** takes up much less space than analogue signals. More space allows for clearer pictures and sound. It also allows for more features, such as programme descriptions, sound in different languages and special services for visually- and hearing-impaired people.

Digital TVs also have space for many more channels. Analogue TVs in the UK only had five channels. Digital TVs have hundreds of channels.

Subtitles help hearing-impaired people read what is being said during a television programme.

digital opposite of analogue; using binary numbers (0s and 1s) in a form that can be used on a computer or television
data information or facts

HIGH-DEFINITION TVS

Companies now make high-definition televisions (HDTVs) to receive digital signals. HDTVs have wide and flat screens. Wider screens give people the feeling that they are watching a cinema screen.

Wide screens can also be larger. In 2014, Samsung launched the largest home TV with a 279-centimetre (110-inch) screen. It cost over £100,000 ($150,000)! Most people can't afford a screen that large, but many have 102- or 127-centimetre (40- or 50-inch) or even larger flat screens in their homes.

HDTVs have wide screens. Many are thin enough to hang on a wall.

SHARPER PICTURES

HDTVs do not use cathode-ray tubes. Instead, they use liquid crystal displays (LCDs) and plasma displays. LCDs pass light through liquid crystals to form images. Plasma displays pass an electric current through a gas-like material called plasma. The plasma shines light on phosphor to create pictures. LCD and plasma TVs create clearer pictures than TVs with cathode-ray tubes.

NEW TECHNOLOGY

TV technology is always changing and improving. Today, some companies make TVs with curved screens. This gives people the feeling that the picture wraps around them, making the viewer feel like he or she is part of the action.

People can also buy 4K TVs (ultra high-definition) and even 3D TVs. Not all TV programmes are suitable for 4K or 3D viewing, but more and more are becoming available to viewers.

TELEVISION ON THE GO

The move from analogue to digital television was the biggest change to television since colour TV was invented in the 1950s. And technology is still changing rapidly. Today, viewers can **stream** television over the Internet. This allows people to watch TV on the go, wherever they can connect to the Internet. Viewers can stream hundreds of television shows and movies on computers, laptops, tablets and even their smartphones.

Today, people can watch TV outside the home on their smartphones or tablets.

stream watch or listen to video or music at the same time that it is being downloaded to your device from the Internet

People can also download TV programmes and films. This means that they can save the programme to their personal device and watch it without an Internet connection.

STAYING CONNECTED

Many people did not own a television 75 years ago. Since then, television has changed our lives. It entertains us. It delivers news. It lets people learn about each other. Television connects people around the world.

Television is one of the main ways people entertain themselves.

TELEVISION TODAY

Today, people watch TV programmes on many different devices, including TVs, computers, smartphones and tablets. This infographic shows that in a 24-hour day, the average person spends more than 10 hours on various electronic devices. More than 5 hours is spent watching television.

Total: 10 hours, 39 minutes

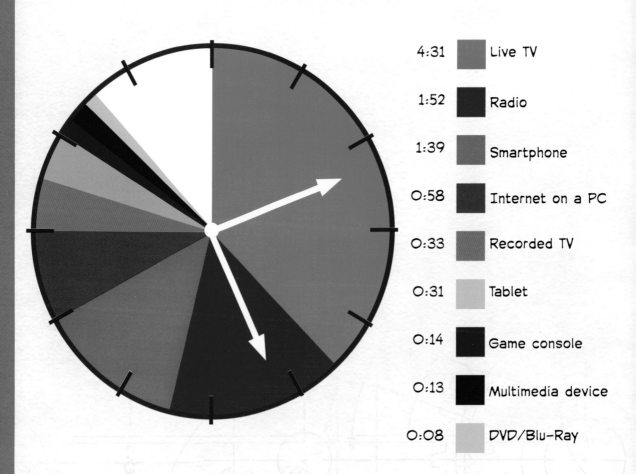

4:31	Live TV
1:52	Radio
1:39	Smartphone
0:58	Internet on a PC
0:33	Recorded TV
0:31	Tablet
0:14	Game console
0:13	Multimedia device
0:08	DVD/Blu-Ray

TIMELINE

1920	The first radio news programme is broadcast in Michigan, USA
1922	The BBC begins broadcasting radio programmes every day
1926	John Logie Baird builds the first mechanical television
1927	The first successful film with sound, *The Jazz Singer*, is made; Philo T. Farnsworth invents a vacuum tube called the image dissector and sends the first electronic television picture
1928	The first mechanical TVs go on sale to the public; Farnsworth demonstrates the first working, entirely electronic television system
1930	Farnsworth receives a patent for his image dissector
1934	The first black-and-white electronic televisions go on sale in Germany
1936	The first electronic televisions go on sale in the UK; the BBC's first live programme, *Here's Looking at You*, is broadcast
1938	Vladimir Zworykin receives a patent for his iconoscope; black-and-white electronic televisions go on sale in the United States
1939	Many people see electronic television for the first time at the New York World's Fair
1939–1945	Television production stops during World War II
1950	The first remote control goes on sale; it is attached to the television by a long wire
1953	The first colour TVs go on sale
1956	The first wireless remote control becomes available
1969	More than half a billion people tune in to watch the Moon landing on television
1971	Subtitles are first displayed at the National Conference on Television for the Hearing Impaired in Tennessee, USA
early 1980s	Subtitles are widely available
2007–2012	The UK makes the switch from analogue to digital television; TVs become available in high-definition and in flat screen
2014	Samsung launches the largest home television – a 279-cm (110-inch) wide screen model

GLOSSARY

analogue opposite of digital; pictures on an analogue TV are made from dots and lines

broadcast send out a programme on TV or radio

data information or facts

digital opposite of analogue; using binary numbers (0s and 1s) in a form that can be used on a computer or television

engineer someone who uses science and maths to design and build things

lunar module self-contained part of the larger spacecraft that landed on the Moon

patent legal document giving sole rights to make or sell a product

receiver device that receives radio signals and turns them into sound or pictures

signal radio, sound or light wave that sends information from one place to another

stream watch or listen to video or music at the same time that it is being downloaded to your device from the Internet

technology use of science to do practical things, such as designing complex machines

vacuum tube glass tube that was used in the past in computers and televisions to control the flow of electricity

variety show show with many different types of performers, such as dancers, singers and comedians

wireless message telegraph message sent over a long distance using radio waves instead of wires

COMPREHENSION QUESTIONS

1. Before television was invented, people entertained themselves in a number of different ways. In what ways has television changed entertainment, for better or worse?

2. Choose two televisions from the book, one early and one modern. Using the text and photos, compare and contrast the two televisions. How has the modern television changed from the early one?

3. In 1969, around half a billion people tuned in to watch American astronauts land on the Moon. Using evidence from the Internet and other sources, what recent events have attracted a huge TV audience?

FIND OUT MORE

10 Ideas that Changed the World, Cath Senker (Wayland, 2016)

Today's Technology (Infographic How it Works), Jon Richards (Wayland, 2016)

The Man Who Invented Television: The Genius of Philo T. Farnsworth (Genius Inventors and Their Great Ideas), Edwin Brit Wyckoff (Enslow Elementary, 2014)

WEBSITES

www.bbc.co.uk/education/clips/zjdy4wx
Find out more about John Logie Baird and the early pioneers of the development of television.

www.dkfindout.com/uk/science/amazing-inventions/television/
Learn more about the development of television technology.

http://kids.britannica.com/kids/article/television/353844#
Learn how televisions work and some of the history of the invention of the television.

INDEX

3D televisions 25

Aldrin, Buzz 4
analogue televisions 20, 21, 23
Apollo 11 4
Armstrong, Neil 4

Baird, John Logie 9, 10, 29
Baird Television Development Company (BTDC) 9
black-and-white televisions 18, 29
British Broadcasting Corporation (BBC) 7, 9, 29

cathode-ray tubes 21, 25
Chaplin, Charlie 8
Circus, The 8
colour televisions 18, 26, 29
curved-screen televisions 25

digital televisions 22–23, 24, 26, 29

electronic televisions 11, 12, 15, 18, 29

Farnsworth, Philo T. 10–11, 12, 15, 16, 29

high-definition televisions (HDTVs) 24, 25, 29
hoop rolling 6

iconoscopes 12, 13, 14, 29
image dissectors 11, 12, 15, 29

Jazz Singer, The 8, 29

Kid, The 8
kinescopes 14

liquid crystal displays (LCDs) 25

mechanical televisions 9, 29
Moon landing 4–5, 29
movies 8, 26, 27, 29

National Broadcasting Company (NBC) 17
National Conference on Television for the Hearing Impaired 18, 29
New York World's Fair 16–17, 29

picture tubes 14
plasma displays 25

Radio Corporation of America (RCA) 15, 17
radios 7
radio signals 10, 11, 12, 14
remote controls 18, 29

streaming 26
subtitles 18, 23, 29

television receivers 14

ultra high-definition (4K) televisions 25

vacuum tubes 14, 29

wireless messages 7
World War II 18, 29
Zworykin, Vladimir 10, 12–14, 15, 16, 29